A Welcome Song for Baby

Especially for Cal, Sarah, Amy, Chris, and all the babies – M.A.
For my sisters, with love – S.A.

A WELCOME SONG FOR BABY
A TAMARIND BOOK 978 1 848 531451
Published in Great Britain by Tamarind,
an imprint of Random House Children's Publishers UK
A Penguin Random House Company

This edition published 2016
1 3 5 7 9 10 8 6 4 2
Text copyright © Marsha Diane Arnold, 2016. Illustrations copyright © Sophie Allsopp, 2016.
The right of Marsha Diane Arnold and Sophie Allsopp to be identified as the author and illustrator
of this work has been asserted in accordance with the Copyright, Designs and Patents Act 1988.
All rights reserved.
RANDOM HOUSE CHILDREN'S PUBLISHERS UK, 61-63 Uxbridge Road, London W5 5SA
www.randomhousechildrens.co.uk www.randomhouse.co.uk
Addresses for companies within The Random House Group Limited can be found at: www.randomhouse.co.uk/offices.htm
THE RANDOM HOUSE GROUP Limited Reg. No. 954009
A CIP catalogue record for this book is available from the British Library.
Printed in China

MIX
Paper from
responsible sources
FSC www.fsc.org FSC® C018179

Penguin Random House is committed to a
sustainable future for our business, our readers
and our planet. This book is made from Forest
Stewardship Council® certified paper.

A Welcome Song for Baby

Marsha Diane Arnold • Sophie Allsopp

Tamarind

Mummy's tummy is growing round — the new baby's coming.
Mummy knits a blanket to welcome the new baby.

Daddy builds the cradle, Grandpa paints the room.
What will I do, I wonder, to welcome the new baby?

One snowy day, we build a snowman in the garden.
Everyone laughs at his funny hat.

"Can the baby hear us, Mummy?" I ask.
"Yes, Emma, the baby is listening."

I whirl in the snow with Higglebee, my bear,
arms stretched to the sky.

"I know what I'll do to welcome the new baby.
I'll share all my favourite sounds!

All the sounds, all round, all round."
Snowflakes whisper in my ear. "Listen, Baby . . .

Winter!

Tinkling icicles. Whistling wind.
Slushity-slush-slush snow.

Chattery teeth. Snowballs SPLOSH.
Sleds and skates shoosh-shooshing.

Purring kitty. Snoring dog.
Pop-pop-crackling fire.

All winter long, I share the sounds.
All the sounds, all round, all round."

Blossom blowing in the breeze.
"Listen, Baby . . .

Spring!

Chirping sparrows. Robin's song.
Dragonflies whirr-whirling.

Clickety bikes. WHOOSHING swings.
Lizards skittle-scooting.

Thunder's rumble. Raindrops' plop.
Mummy's silvery night songs.

All spring long, I share the sounds.
All the sounds, all round, all round."

Swallows singing to the sky.
"Listen, Baby . . .

Summer!

Hum-hummy bees. Buzzy flies.
Crickets zip-zeep-zeeping.

BOING bouncy balls. Skipping chants.
Sprinklers sput-spit-sputtering.

Croa...OAKING froggies. Hooting owls.
Daddy's campfire stories.

All summer long, I share the sounds.
All the sounds, all round, all round."

Now, I hum a hurry, hurry bee song
as we wait . . .

Suddenly, Mummy sits up straight.
"Emma, call your daddy.
Today is Baby's birth day."

Mummy and Daddy hurry out the door.

Grandpa, Higglebee and I
wait and wait and wait . . .

Until happy cries sing out

and fill our house,
from Mummy, Daddy, Grandpa, me . . .

and
Baby!

...leaves swish swooshing, squeaky mouse,

honking geese above us...

"Listen, Baby . . . *Autumn.*"